CHASKA
AND THE
GOLDEN DOLL

This story is dedicated to all the children of the Andes.
May their dreams someday come true.

First Edition

Library of Congress Cataloging-in-Publication Data

Alexander, Ellen.

Chaska and the golden doll / by Ellen Alexander. —1st ed.

p. cm.

ISBN 1-55970-241-9

1. Indians of South America—Peru—Cuzco (Province)—Social life and customs—Juvenile literature. 2. Incas—Antiquities—Juvenile literature. 3. Cuzco (Peru : Province)—Antiquities—Juvenile literature. [1. Indians of South America—Andes Region—Social life and customs. 2. Incas—Antiquities.] I. Title.

F3429.1.C9A52   1994

985' .3701—dc20   93-34691

Published in the United States by Arcade Publishing, Inc., New York

Distributed by Little, Brown and Company

10 9 8 7 6 5 4 3 2 1

Designed by Abby Kagan

IMAGO

Printed in China

CHASKA
AND THE
GOLDEN DOLL

BY ELLEN ALEXANDER

ARCADE PUBLISHING · NEW YORK

Chaska stood alone by the side of the road. She saw her father working in the field below. She watched the boys and a few of the older girls hurrying past her on their way to school. And all around, the great snow peaks of the Andes shone in the morning sun.

Chaska wondered how it would be to sit at one of the long wooden desks in the schoolhouse. She dreamed of writing her name, and of reading books with stories and pictures in them. But she could only dream. The village didn't have enough money to build a school large enough for all the children.

Wandering to the courtyard, Chaska found her mother and grandfather stripping maize. They pulled the golden kernels from the cobs and put them into bags to send to market.

Chaska loved to sit with Grandfather and listen to his stories of long ago. His grandparents and their grandparents had lived here in the Sacred Valley of the Incas.

"Look, Chaskita," said Grandfather. "See how the sun turns the maize into Inca gold?"

Chaska asked him to tell her again about Papa Inti, Sun God of the Incas.

"Long ago," he began, "when the people called Incas lived here, Papa Inti ruled the world. When he got too hot, he started to sweat, and the drops fell to earth as gold. The Incas worked the gold into forms like the ones they found in the world around them. They made these golden idols to honor Papa Inti, for this was *his* gold, and this was *his* world.

"The Incas kept most of the gold near here, in the city of Cuzco," continued Grandfather. "There they built a temple for Papa Inti, with a garden of gold inside. Golden trees," he told Chaska, "and golden animals, too…"

"Even the grass? And the birds in the trees?"

"Yes. And golden eggs in golden nests that glittered and shone like the Sun God himself. Then strangers from a distant land came and stole the gold. They took all but a few little pieces. The Incas managed to hide those inside their houses of stone in these mountains around us."

They looked up at the mountains. The shadows told them it was time to gather kindling for the dinner fire. The two started up the mountainside together. Kusi, the puppy, went running ahead.

They climbed past the fields of maize and wheat; past cows, and horses, and llamas. They crossed stone terraces and old stone walls that once formed the homes of the Inca people.

The sun grew hotter. The air grew thinner. Grandfather felt tired and stopped to rest in the shade. But Chaska and Kusi went in search of adventure among the ancient walls.

Kusi found a rabbit hole and started digging, sending showers of earth and stones into the air. One of the stones, touched by the sun, caught Chaska's attention. She picked it up and cried, "Oh, Kusi! This isn't a stone....It's a doll!"

The doll was small and heavy and smooth. It glowed like the sun itself.

"Grandfather! Grandfather! Look what we found! A little golden doll!"

Grandfather's eyes grew wide.

"Yes, Chaskita. This is indeed real gold! But it is more than a doll. What you have found is an Inca idol!" Then softly he added, "Papa Inti has given you this gift because you are a daughter of the Incas."

They gazed in wonder at the little idol.

"According to the laws of our village," Grandfather explained, "the idol is yours to keep. Papa Inti has led you to it for a reason. Now you must try to think what that reason can be. To give you something you want? To make some wish come true?"

As they walked home, Chaska thought very hard. She thought about all the things she might like. A new dress? New shoes? Some paper and crayons? Maybe she would just keep the doll as a plaything.

She thought and thought as she washed the doll in the stream by her home. She thought some more as she polished it clean. By the time she went into the house, she knew what her wish must be.

Inside, the dinner fire blazed. It gleamed in the eyes of the chickens, rabbits, and guinea pigs huddled against the dark walls. Sweet eucalyptus smoke filled the stone kitchen. Through the smoke came Grandfather's voice.

"Chaskita. Have you thought well about your gift from Papa Inti?"

The fire crackled. Chaska was silent. Then, almost in a whisper, she answered, "Grandfather, I want to write words and read books. I want to learn about the Inca people."

Grandfather nodded and slowly smiled. "I think the idol will help you get your wish. Tomorrow I will speak to the Council of Elders."

The members of the council were old and wise. Everyone in the village respected their suggestions. After listening to Grandfather's story, they came up with a plan. They suggested that Chaska sell the idol to the Inca Museum in Cuzco. The money could be used to enlarge the school so Chaska and all the other children could go.

The next day, Chaska's whole family went to the city of
Cuzco. They rode for hours in an old pickup truck, stopping for
passengers along the way.

When they reached Cuzco, they climbed to the museum
where the Inca treasures were kept.

The museum directors were glad to buy the golden idol.
They put it into a lighted glass case where everyone could see it.
Chaska and her family felt very proud.

When they returned home, they told the whole village of
their plans for a new schoolhouse. Everyone wanted to help. They
dug the foundation. They sawed and hammered. In a few weeks,
the building was finished.

A great festival took place at the new school. There were sweets and a huge pot of chicken soup. Musicians played and people danced. They celebrated all night long and thanked Chaska for sharing her good fortune with them.

And in the days that followed, Chaska thanked Papa Inti for helping her dream-wish come true.

A Note on the Story

Chaska and her family are real people. They live in a tiny village in the Sacred Valley near Cuzco, Peru. Most of the villages in the region have not been so lucky as Chaska's. Some have schools too small to hold all the children, and others have no schools at all.